Business in Bangkok

by
Lynn Westerhout

Illustrated by
Chum McLeod

Second
Story
Press

When Corey's mom came home from work, she gave him an extra-special big hug.

"I will miss you when I am in Bangkok," she said.

"What's Bangkok?" asked Corey.

"It's a city in Thailand," said Corey's dad. "Mommy has to fly there for work. She will be away ten days."

"Ten days!" cried Corey. "She can't go to Bangkok for ten days."

"Why not?" asked Corey's dad. "People do."

"People do," said Corey. "But not Mommy. Mommy can't go."

"**W**ho will make my lunch?"

"Well, I could," said Corey's dad.

"I always make breakfast so I could make your lunch. But … so could you."

"**W**ho will tie my laces?"

"I could, but ... so could you."

"**W**ho will fix my bear?"

"I could, but ... so could you."

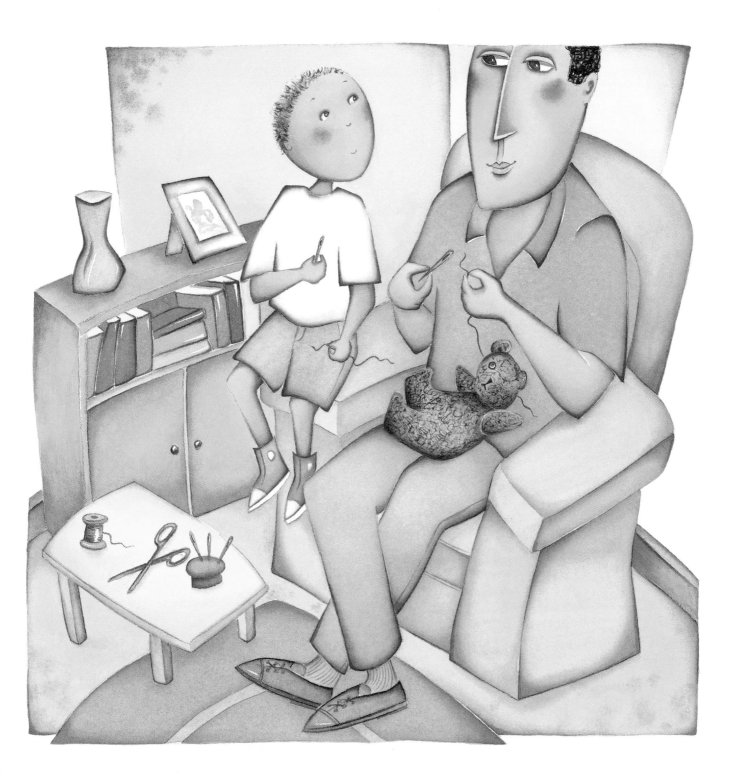

"Who will iron my best shirt?"

"I will, just like always. But you can help."

"**W**ho will scrub my back in the bath?"

"I could," said Corey's dad, "but ... so could you."

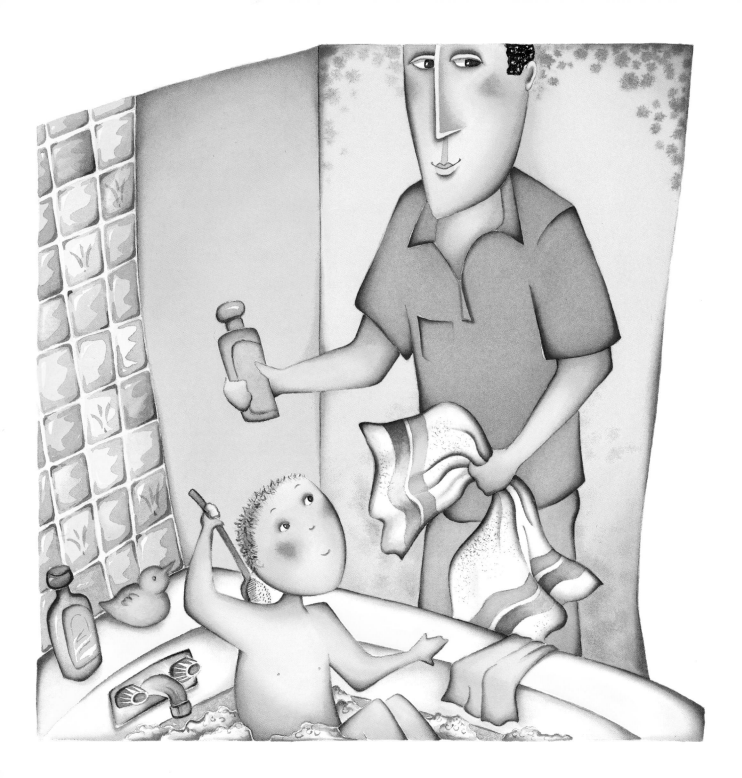

"Who will put on my pyjamas?"

"You will, just like always."

"Who will give me a hug?"

"I will always give you hugs.
Great big bristle hugs. Here's one,
and another and another!"

"But who will give me Mommyhugs?"

"Only Mommy can do that. Look, she's thinking about you, too. She's sent you something special."

"I can read this myself.

Dear Corey,
I owe you ten hugs. One for each
day I am away. I miss you.
Love, Mommy."

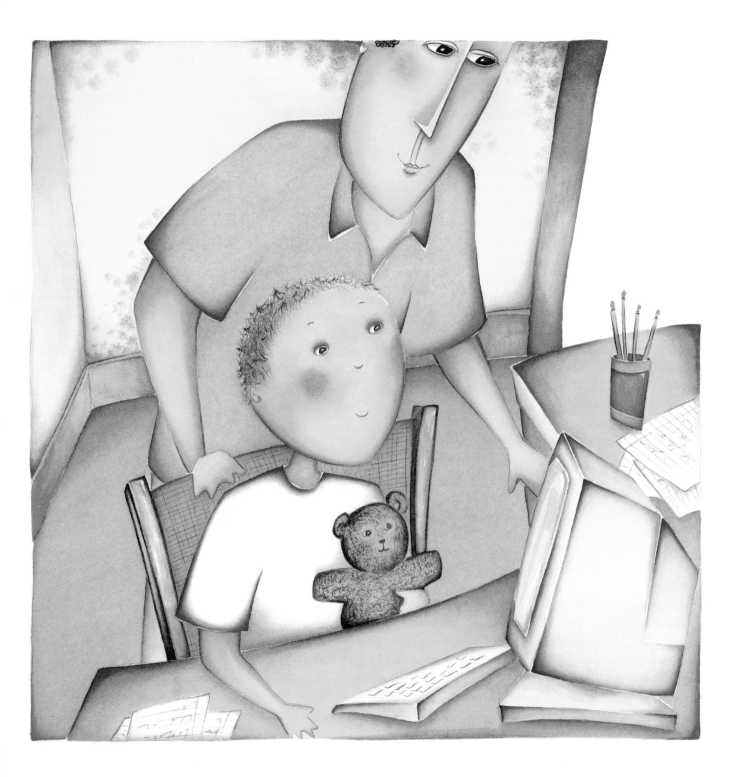

So what did Corey's mom give him the moment she arrived?

The ten biggest and best Mommyhugs in the whole world and a big kiss, too.

National Library of Canada Cataloguing in Publication Data

Westerhout, Lynn, 1952-
Business in Bangkok

ISBN 1-896764-48-7

I. McLeod, Chum. II. Title

PS8595.E6953B88 2001   jC813'.6   C2001-901347-7
PZ7.W51967Bu 2001

Printed and bound in Hong Kong, China
by Book Art Inc., Toronto

*Second Story Press gratefully acknowledges the support of the
Ontario Arts Council and the Canada Council for the Arts for our publishing program.
We acknowledge the financial support of the Government of Canada through the
Book Publishing Industry Development Program.*

Published by
SECOND STORY PRESS
720 Bathurst Street, Suite 301
Toronto, Canada
M5S 2R4

www.secondstorypress.on.ca